Lost Soul

By Rayne Havok

Published by Rayne Havok
Copyright © December 2021 & April 2022
By Rayne Havok

All rights reserved

This is a work of fiction, if you find similarities, they are coincidental. No part of this book can be reproduced, copied, or sold without consent from the author.

May Offend

Although, not like anything I've written before, there may still be triggering moments.

For first time readers, please know that this is not my normal genre of writing and read the others with caution.

One

May

Get up... just get the fuck up.

Pleading with myself to just get out of bed in the morning is an exhausting part of my day. There is nothing to wake up for, nothing awaiting my attention, just more... *nothing*.

The hollow pit in my chest, the ache in my throat, the numbness throughout my body; all constant. The thing that finally calls loud enough to be answered is the incessant urgency to pee. *Fucking human needs.*

Dragging my feet to the bathroom, it feels like a mountain has erected itself through the floorboards in the middle of my bedroom, and now I must get over it.

I go through the customary morning things; working on auto-pilot. Dragging the brush through my hair hard enough to bring tears to my eyes, I tell my reflection to fuck off and pull harder just for spite. The burning hatred, the thing that loves to see me hurt, creeps forward, encouraging me, daring me.

I let the brush fall to the floor on the last pull through my ratted nest. I look no different now than when I walked in here, just missing a few clumps of hair.

    Stumbling back through the master bedroom, I grab my sweater off the treadmill—which had all the hopes of being used as something other than a coat rack, and pull it on, leaving the hood haphazardly atop my head. I slip into shoes I hope match, but cannot care if they don't, then leave through the front door. Not bothering to lock it, I will have no use for this shithole beyond today—my last day on earth.

    I hadn't checked the clock before I left, but from the look of the neighborhood, it feels late-afternoon. Just enough cars outside of their houses to indicate the earlier shifts have gotten home, but not late enough for the overachievers.

    It's chillier than I thought it would be, autumn creeping in. I pull my sleeves over my hands to use as gloves, and push forward; not having a clear directive today, just letting my feet fall where they may.

    Walking slowly through the park I had played in as a child, I note the differences in landscape, but nothing's changed with the playground equipment. *Cheap bastards.* I bet these kids are getting the same splinters and cuts I had grown accustomed to in my youth.

    Kicking through the sand box I can't be bothered to walk around, I become only mildly annoyed when my shoes fill with the earth.

I trudge along, eyes on the ground, watching in amazement as my feet seem to carry me without any real thought to direction. I look up when I realize they've stopped. It turns out they must have known what they were doing this whole time.

I'm just inches from standing on the graves of my parents, buried together for god knows what reason—maybe a discounted rate or something.

I don't remember feeling like I needed one final goodbye with them, but I'm here, so my feet must have known something I hadn't pieced together.

I plop on the ground and read the large stone they share across two plots like I hadn't done it before. *Leaving behind a beautiful daughter.*

I wonder, again, who had thought that phrase should be carved there. My parents certainly hadn't ever uttered those words to me before.

In fact, I can recall the last words my father said, with reference to me, on his last night on earth. *"You take her, I got better things to worry about."* And then I'd watched as he walked out the door, a suitcase in hand, and a shoulder bag slung across his chest. He hadn't even said goodbye. He was leaving us for a lady he'd been having an affair with at work, crashing his car before he had even gotten to her.

I would relive the story countless times in the alcohol fumes of my mother's mouth throughout the years.

I am unable to form words to say to them, and soon the silence distracts me, like it often does, lulling me into oblivion. I am startled into alertness by the sudden appearance of a stranger laying flowers on a grave in the row ahead of me.

I watch him pay his respects, curious what the customary protocol actually was. He is quiet with his words, but I can feel the emotion in the harshness of his whispers—heartbroken and sad.

He stands up from his crouch and touches the headstone gently with his fingertips as if it were the actual person in the ground, then walks away without a glance in my direction.

I guess mourning is a solitary thing.

Not that I *wanted* to show my half-assed attempt at a friendly smile, my I'm-sorry-for-your-loss smile, but it irks me that he is alright not offering me one, he couldn't know I am an empty vessel of a human with no feelings to fill the void.

I could have been really sad over here, and he hadn't cared.

And I'm the worthless one.

Most people are overflowing with emotions, but unable to share them. Unwilling to risk them on another person; to be honest about them. Too afraid they may get hurt.

I'm often jealous that they have them to give but won't share, while what little I can conjure is offered, but most likely not treasured like the gift it was given.

Anyway, enough of that talk. I'm on the last leg of my trek now, no use getting riled up. I get to my feet, walk to their head stone, and before I know what I'm doing, I place my hand on it gently and tap it in the same manner I'd witnessed earlier.

I do not have some sort of emotional breakthrough and it disappoints me that I couldn't have a moment of peace with them.

My feet take me before I think them to, weaving me through the cemetery and out to the main road. I watch the cars speeding toward whatever awaits them at their destination, fascinated that they could be excited for such things: wives, husbands, kids, pets; something that claims their attention. I am merely an obstacle that needs to be avoided, so I stay on the sidewalk, leaving them free to concentrate on other things; liking it best when people don't fuss over me.

I follow the curve of the road, over the steep incline that will take me to the highest point in town. Leading me to the bridge; my last stop of the day, or my life… whatever. Looking around as I arrive, I note that I'm the only one who has made this journey tonight, not that it is usually bustling, but it's empty tonight, save for me.

I amble right up to the edge and look down; I have done this countless times; no real conviction in the task. But tonight, as darkness falls around me, I am ready to go.

Today had been my last day for months now. Having chosen a random date out of my head saved me the wonderment of when it may happen and gave me something to look forward to.

I catch a few of the newly falling rain pellets on my cheek and look to the sky for others. It's not unusual to have the rain start up out of the blue during this season, so I don't take it as a sign from the heavens.

Opening my mouth to the quickening drops, I taste the earth-flavored liquid. I let it wash me, saturate me, quench me. And then, before I even know I have decided to go, I have gone. My torso folding forward, the momentum of my shifting weight pulling me over the railing.

Two

Zachary

I clutch my chest, sadness crippling me to my core. Never having felt a pull stronger than this, I beg my eyes to focus on the bright purple light, the light that is crying out its tortured tears.

Moving as fast as I can to get there in time, pulling up just short of her—the girl on the bridge—the one who's ready to let it all go. I can sense her determination; her finality in this decision. Her emptiness has ripped me in half.

She has her face cast upward, her arms crucifixion-style. The light, that is supposed to be inside her, mingling within her body, is leeching out; seeping from her human form.

I have never seen anything like it. The body must die before the soul can leave. But this girl is standing in front of me, I know she isn't dead, and yet I can see her soul escaping.

I watch her body shift and then bend forward. Before I can catch myself, a sob erupts from my chest as I watch the hazy purple light go over.

There's a long moment before I can stop my agonizing screams, until I can see that it was *only* the light. The girl is still standing there, but now, her eyes are on mine.

Three

May

I catch myself just before the pivotal moment of my freefall, caught off guard by the animalistic cry ripping through the air, burying deep into my ears, I'm stunned motionless.

I watch as this man heaves, gut-wrenching noises screaming from his chest. I have never seen so much passion for anything. *Ever*. And he seems to be reacting to me and my… situation.

I'm stunned, immobile, unable to even right myself. Leaning my head onto the ledge, I use it to support me. My legs begin to shake and my hands tremble. My vision pulsates with darkness behind my eyes, flooding with the rush of blood through my veins. My breath is heavy.

I catch his eyes before I crumble. His arms take hold around my waist as he pulls me against his chest.

I try to focus on something other than my own weakening strength as I struggle to remain upright.

His chest is drawing deep, searching for air, presumably trying to recover from his… episode.

He pulls me into more of an embrace, I'm trying to reciprocate but my body is unable to follow any command.

"Shh," he breathes onto the top of my head. "You're full of adrenaline, this is going to pass; the blood just needs to get back in order."

I focus on the rocking of his body, moving like he is soothing a small child. I surrender myself to the hypnotic motion, and after a while, my legs are sturdy on the ground and I'm able to support my own weight again. That fact does not seem to register to this man, it seems he may need this hug more than me now.

Testing my arms for strength, like my legs, they seem to have gotten their receptors back, I'm compelled to hug him just as fiercely as he is me—feeling safe and warm, I want to return that to him.

I let myself feel his strength and I mirror it, wrapping my arms around his waist, I grip my hands together where they meet, and hold him tightly. Which in turn causes him to pull tighter; like some sort of one-upmanship: hug edition. I know I've met the extent of my squeeze capacity, so I let him win.

He smells like the warm rain, and before I can stop myself, I'm taking a deep cleansing breath which enables me to relax further into his embrace. I almost feel like I did before I half-jumped off the bridge.

His hands loosen and start to move up and down my back, a mixture of both caress and groping massage.

I let out a slow, stuttering breath that comes more audibly like a moan.

He doesn't seem to notice, and it feels too good to wonder any further what it meant, so I let my tensions go and just feel.

Being numb for so long had dulled my senses but it feels as though he is opening up every nerve and putting his finger prints on them. My own left grasping the back of his shirt for no other reason than the need to squeeze something.

The rain has disappeared and it left a cold breeze in its wake, only the parts of me not touching this stranger are cold though. The goosebumps finally build momentum and a shiver runs across my body.

"Come on, I'll get you home." He pulls me away from him but instantly wraps me back into his one-armed embrace, walking with me in the direction I lead.

I have given no thought to what it means that I am perfectly content to bring this man to my house, but I have no trepidation. I walk him right up to the front door and he pauses. "Do you have your key?"

I shrug my shoulders and push the door open. "Didn't think I'd need any of this stuff after…," I leave the rest of the sentence on my tongue.

He pulls me up the stairs, assuming correctly that the bedrooms are up here, taking my lead when he becomes unsure where to go next. I stand just inside the door awaiting further instruction, not really understanding why I need them.

"Let's get you into some dry clothes."

"Ok." I go about finding something warm and dry to wear; changing just inside my closet.

"I don't have anything that will fit you…," I stop abruptly, realizing that not only is he dry, he is also clean—as though we hadn't just trudged across town through muc puddles.

I know I should be trying to understand how this is true, but I don't have the mental strength for rationalizing, and I can't think of a feasible reason for it to be—but it is, so, I leave it at that. Forgotten the second I let it free of my mind.

I curl up in bed after he pulls the covers down and then I close my eyes as he tucks me into them without getting inside them himself. "You can sleep with me," I mumble.

"I don't sleep." Is what it sounds like he says, but that can't be true, it doesn't make sense. I am asleep before I can formulate another thought.

Four

Zachary

I watch her intently while she falls asleep. I'm shocked at the night's events. Things that shouldn't be possible have very clearly happened. She should not be alive, or rather, she should, but her soul should still be inside of her. Had I not fucked up, she would have gone over the bridge like she had intended. I would have been there to point her soul to her traumas, gotten her to face them—and heal from them, leaving her soul to repair itself and be able to move on.

But I had to be so *reactive*, so thoughtless. I know what I have to do. I just can't think of that right now. Not with her so close, and my response to her so personal.

I've let her down, the disappointment I feel for myself is immense.

I try and hold on to the feeling of her soul's purple light, dimming quickly as time passes. I can feel it, gloomy with stress, lost without a guide or escort to point it toward its path.

I push up the wall and come to my feet, walking over to her dresser, I touch all the little bottles and trinkets, dusty from neglect. I pick up a small frame, a picture of this girl at a younger time—and the only photo around. I notice she is not smiling like most young children do, toothy and wide, with the knowledge of a shitty world not yet learned. Blissful.

The girl in the photo, with sad eyes, has learned such lessons. My throat tightens and I can feel the threat of tears stinging my eyes.

Carefully, I place the frame back on the dresser, making sure to nestle it right into the dust-free spot of wood it sat before.

I walk around the perimeter of her room, noticing little things here and there that remind me of my own life. A very clear image of a sad and lonely existence, evident in every facet of her world, knowing from experience what to look for.

I can't help but touch, I want to be close to her, touch anything she has. So, I do, walking the full house, I touch everything. Running my fingers over every surface, not minding the dust loosening its grip on the furniture and becoming air born. I absorb all the knowledge I can from reading what her house tells me.

I make it back to her room, the sun finally shining in the sky, marking the start of the day. She has tossed the covers off and is mumbling something I can't understand. On instinct, I walk to her side, crouch to her level, and smooth my hand softly through her hair.

Five

May

I bolt upright, out of what I can only vaguely remember to be a nightmare, one of many I cycle through during my nights. The threat of being touched while I sleep weighs heavier on my mind then, making it impossible to rest.

    I look into my stranger's eyes, seeing instantly the shock I must have caused him written clearly on his face.

    "Sorry, love, didn't mean to scare you."

    "It's ok, just don't like being touched while I sleep." I try to smile a reassurance at him, but his face remains hesitant.

    I climb out of my bed, a little surprised by the ease of it. It usually takes an argument from my mind to extricate myself from my cocoon.

    Chalking it up to a random event, I walk to the bathroom. I'm not really sure what to do, since yesterday I was technically supposed to be dead. This feels like a mark in time that I should value, as though the countdown ended. Maybe I can start the timer over. Like a new car with zero miles on it, instead of the one I had been inside, running on fumes.

I pick my brush up off the floor and look at myself in the mirror. My hair is wild, making it hard to settle on a place to start detangling it.

The clear magnitude of what actually happened yesterday is evident on every inch of my face, a face I haven't looked at in intricate detail for so long. My cheekbones look hollow, my royal blue eyes, dimmed to a foggy sky. The bruise-colored bags underneath them, more prominent than they'd ever been. My lips, chapped from a night spent in the rain. I run my tongue across the sloughing skin, trying to return the moisture.

Feeling dirty from my little adventure, I turn the shower on and step in. I wash my hair—twice, hoping it will help loosen the knots so I can run the brush through it. Washing my face, trying to give it life. I don't remember the last time I showered so thoroughly, usually it's treated like more a task to mark off than an actual necessity.

I pull a clean towel from under the sink and wrap it around myself. I comb my hair, wincing when I catch a tangle. I'm surprised when I notice myself taking care not to do it again, not feeling the need to cause myself pain—that's new for me.

After finishing the mess on my head, I notice how long my hair has become. I can't actually recall the last time I'd had it cut. *Years?* Maybe.

I glance at the man sitting on my bed as I cross to the closet for fresh clothes. "What's your name?" I say, not stopping until I'm hidden behind the door where I drop my towel and pull on a mostly-clean shirt over my head.

He doesn't answer until I'm dressed and back in the room with him. I had mostly assumed he hadn't heard me.

"Z...Zachary?" I hear the question mark behind his answer.

"You sure?" An unfamiliar sound comes out of my mouth and I realize I just chuckled.

"It's been a while since I thought about it."

"Not usually something one needs to think about." I watch him struggle to pull a response together. He looks uncomfortable so I offer him a reprieve. "I'm May."

"Nice to meet you, May."

"Do you want coffee? I don't have food; didn't really think I'd need it anymore." I see the words as they hit him, the gravity of what they mean. I'm surprised that *I* also wince.

"Sure, thank you."

I lead him downstairs and put together our drinks. "I don't have sugar or anything," I add as an afterthought, setting his cup in front of him.

"You know I would have taken the plastic one had I known." He is talking about me drinking mine from a disposable, red solo cup.

"You're the guest, you can use the mug." I feel a hint of sadness that I only have one mug, the implications of that hit me hard. I swallow a sip and it gets caught in my throat, swollen with the emotion.

I have lived with depression all my life. People often understand that to mean the sufferer would be sad most of the time. For me, it means that I actually don't feel much of anything, sort of numb, hollow. *Vacant.*

The fact that I am feeling *anything* is startling to me, and even though they are sad feelings, at least it's something. It's kind of nice. I take another sip of the hot drink, tasting it; *actually* tasting it, which is another thing to add to the list of 'new'.

I sit back and watch Zachary, he's looking right at me, but I don't feel a need to turn away. My eyes follow his arm as it brings the mug to his mouth and then back to the table again. I watch his throat as it works the liquid; bobbing to complete the task.

His eyes are like crystal, so blue they radiate. Soft blond hair, a little messy on top of his head, but short around his ears. A few days of stubble across his jaw. Full lips, distractingly so. He must notice my pause, and I watch him pull his bottom lip into his mouth. Nothing sexual about it, just one of those things we all do subconsciously under scrutiny. It comes out wet and I think about the taste of it. My mouth goes dry and I become thirsty for him.

Full minutes pass before I'm fully aware that time is moving, accustomed to sitting still in thought regularly, I rarely pay attention. "Thank you," I have to clear my throat before I can finish, arousal blocking the words this time. "For getting me home last night." My tongue works nervously around my lips, thinking about his on mine, unable to hold it still, I let it roam.

"I'm glad I could help." He is watching me; his eyes get squinty with thought.

"What?" I ask, because I need to know.

"That was really hard for me to see."

I can see the pain in his eyes as he is obviously recalling what happened at the bridge. "I'm sorry." I don't know what else to say.

"Don't apologize for that," he says, adamantly.

"I'm sor…" I cut myself off before I can apologize for my apology. *Man, this human interaction thing is hard.*

He smiles at my effort. "Thank you."

"So, Zachary, what were you doing there last night? On the bridge, I mean." I take a sip of my drink hiding my face and watching his over the rim of the cup. His squinty, thinking-eyes are back.

"I saw that you needed help," he says, hesitantly.

I just nod my head, unsure what to say.

"I'm sorry I was too late... or too early." He seems to catch on that his words have confused me. "I'm sorry, I don't know..." He waves his hands around animatedly. "It's all too much."

I can feel the sadness of his words. Putting myself in his shoes, I imagine it would be hard to watch someone end their life. "Thank you for caring."

He tries to compose himself, gives me a generic smile, one that doesn't reach his eyes—that's where you find his truths, you've got to listen to his eyes, and they say he isn't over it.

I try to continue, thinking about how normal people would converse, I say, "Do you go there often... to the bridge, I mean. It's pretty up there." I put my pinky nail in my mouth, a nervous habit returning.

"I do, I sort of work there."

"Oh, nice."

Six

Zachary

I have to tell her. I know she needs to hear it—and the sooner the better. But I've never actually had to tell someone what I do, by the time they meet me, it's usually obvious.

I try to formulate the words so I don't scare her, testing them in my head first, hearing the ridiculousness of them in any order, I go for it and blurt it out. "I help people." I watch her nod. "People like you," I add.

She raises an eyebrow. "Like a suicide prevention sort of thing? You watch the bridge looking for *people like me*?"

"Not quite prevention."

"What, you do clean up then?"

I can tell her words affect her. "No. Not the humanly clean up, anyway. I kind of help your soul navigate. Help it see."

She laughs. "Okaaay."

"It can be confusing, and even more so when it's a suicide. It's kind of a shocking thing."

She leans forward, putting her chin in her hands and elbows on the table.

I continue, "So, when you die the soul leaves the human form. It has a kind of journey to complete. Depending on your life, it may be an easy one. Most suicides are not the case. So many traumas harden the soul—callusing it."

"Ok."

"So, *your* soul…"

"*My* soul?"

She looks as confused as I feel, having to explain it to her. "Is not intact." I wait for it to sink in. She waves her hands for me to continue, assuming I'll clear up what she thinks she misunderstood. "I watched your soul. It made the jump."

"Because you can see them… and you saw mine jump… without me." She looks skeptical as she fills in the blanks sarcastically.

"Yes."

"Obviously." She sucks her teeth, making a loud noise. "Well, I am either going to ask you to leave now, or you can do a better job of making this little thing believable." She holds my eyes with hers, expectantly, eyebrow cocked, lips pursed.

"Maybe I could tell you my story?" I ask. She nods her head, folding her arms across her chest and leans back into the chair.

I take a deep breath. I haven't told this story before, not completely, anyway. "Well, I had always suffered with depression, though at the time it wasn't called that."

She stops me. "*At the time?*"

I can see her confusion. We do look the same age. I pick up where I left off, not wanting to lose momentum. "I think it was 1948 when I was... *alive.*"

"Aww, of course." Even with her sarcasm, I can see some part of her believes me.

"Anyway, I was sadder than most, withdrawn, lonely to the point of despair. My parents couldn't help me, they tried, in vain, to love me more, nurture me more. Nothing helped. We weren't wealthy, doctors and other avenues weren't an option. I would hurt myself, claw and scratch my skin. It worried my parents, but I couldn't stop, it was the only thing I felt. In fact, it became like a compulsion, I couldn't stop thinking about that feeling. About *actually* feeling. Then I began to cut myself." I pull her arm free from her chest and lift the sleeve of her shirt above her wrist. "I noticed that we share that."

She pulls another fake smile and tugs her arm free. "Go on."

"As you know, it can be quite hard to explain to somebody why you would be the one who has hurt yourself. How hard it is to explain the physical *need* to do it. My parents must have thought I was crazy. On occasion, I had cut too deeply and my father had to stitch me himself; fearing what the neighbors would think if they'd found out. I became a recluse, afraid for my parents' sake, not wanting them shamed for my compulsions."

I can see she relates to my words and she gives me a tentative smile.

I try to return it but the story has me thinking about those times. "Later, I became sort of attracted to the girl next door, mostly due to proximity, I think. She was a few years older and kind of a loner herself. I would watch her sometimes. Curious really. She'd caught me once and told me she would have sex with me. I was shocked, but I didn't refuse the offer. It was awkward, rushed, and made me feel bad. We didn't talk for months after that.

"She came to me one afternoon; actually sought me out. I was trying to think of a way to let her down easy, not wanting a repeat of what we had done. She told me she was pregnant. I was fifteen, didn't even know it could happen at that age.

"We had a baby girl. Sofia. Beautiful little white-haired girl. Perfect. She and her family said she couldn't keep her, that she had too much potential to ruin it with a child.

"I wanted that baby more than anything, the second I'd learned of the pregnancy. My parents helped me with her after she moved in with us. I think it's called SIDS now… sudden infant death syndrome. She lived ninety-five days." I watch May wipe tears from her eyes and I pause to swallow my own down.

"I went in one morning to wake Sofia for the day. She was already gone; I could tell just by looking at her." The memory of her, a shade too blue for life, rushes in.

"I lost it. She was the only thing that had ever elicited a reaction from me; my little blond light.

"We had a small funeral for her: my mother, father and me. No one else really knew her to attend. I told her mother, who'd said it was for the best. Can you fucking *believe* that? *The fucking best!*

"It hurt me to know that her own mother hadn't loved her. Just my parents and I were all she had in this world. I didn't feel like it was enough. Sofia deserved to have people worshipping at her feet; my little princess."

"You loved her very much, that was enough."

I chuff. "Well," I continue, not wanting to argue. "I pretty much spun out of control from there. I left home, ran away from anything that reminded me of my loss. I lived eight hard years on the streets. Never went back home, never talked to my parents again. I lost myself in my misery. I went over the bridge too." I see her brow furrow.

"*That* bridge?"

I nod my confirmation. "The very same."

Seven

May

What the fuck? "Sooo, you're dead?" I ask, still in the middle of trying to understand this whole thing.

He nods again. "I don't really know what most souls do after they pass. I guess they can do anything they want. I chose to help the suicide souls find their path. It can be a hard journey."

"And mine is out there, like you say, wandering?"

"Yes. I can hear it."

"You can hear souls?"

"Not usually. I think I had a strong connection to yours. Hence my reaction to what happened."

How could I forget? His cries, the single worst thing I have ever heard in my life. "So, why don't we just go find it, see if we can cram it back in me?" I ask, only half serious, I don't think that's how this works, although, it had left without my death. *So maybe?*

"No, it won't work that way. Sorry." His face falls with regret.

"Well, fuck, this is a lot to take in."

"I know. There is more that we should get through though. It's important."

"Oh, great." My sarcasm seeps out again.

"So we kind of have to *right* what has gone wrong here."

"Which would be my lack of soul, and my inability to shove it back in."

"Exactly." He takes a while to say his next words, but I can tell he is thinking it over by all the muscle ticks his face is doing. His teeth let go of the inside of his cheek and he says, "I am assuming you are a strong woman; that you can hear this, and we can work on how to get it done together."

"I do think I've taken what we've gone over so far pretty well."

"This is worse."

He seems to wait for conformation that I am, in fact, a big girl who can hear this, so I nod.

"Your soul is dimming, sort of losing strength. It is stagnant, being tethered by your body. It can't let go, or move forward."

"Ok."

"If we don't sever the connection, and soon, it will be lost to the darkness."

"And how would we *sever* that connection?"

Zachary takes a shaky breath that worries me to my core and he says, "You will have to die."

"Aww." Well, isn't that the most ironic thing? Any other point in my life I would have seen nothing sad about this. But now. Here. Feeling things. I don't want to go.

Both lost in thought, we sit in silence. My mind is running wild with regret, they do say that a large percentage of people who have attempted suicide actually regret it and are happy that it was not a success. Before this, I could not have understood that.

"How?" I blurt out.

"*How?* How will you have to die? Is that what you're asking?"

I nod, putting my finger nail in my mouth.

"You have to kill your body."

"Me?" I squeak.

"It has to be you."

"Why? I don't want to do it anymore."

"May, if I could do this for you, I would. But I don't have the power to take a life."

"Well, maybe I could get someone else to do it."

"The people out there don't see you anymore. Their souls won't recognize an empty body. Nothing they could do to you would kill you."

"People don't see me anymore?" I mean I didn't think they ever did. But now they *really* don't. "But I see you, is that because you don't have a soul either?"

"I suppose so, could be. I don't see anyone else like I see you. And no one else sees me."

I don't know why his words mean so much to me. Leave it to me to take them and twist them out of context, making up some love story.

"Like I said, I think the connection was formed."

This whole thing just has me flustered and confused. "Ok, then, let me get this straight. My soul is lost, I'm here—my body anyway. I have to die so it will not be lost anymore. But once it's found, it won't recognize anyone? It will be alone again?"

"Souls don't really need anyone; they aren't lacking a connection. We are all sort of… everything, not really discernable from anyone else. It's not as lonely as you might think."

"But I won't recognize you anymore… specifically." I don't care that I sound desperate right now.

"No, once your body is… dead…your soul will get a sort of beacon, a light, it will follow through the steps to cleanse it; healing it, in a way. Then it will be free. And One with everything else."

"Oh."

"I would want to know you… after. If I could, if it *were* possible, I'd like nothing more." He looks at my face, his eyes ticking over it: from eyes, to nose, to cheek, to mouth.

There goes that subconscious tongue thing again. I taste my lip and watch him take a deep breath. I'm not very good at this, but I can see he would like to kiss me. I blush, heat burning from my chest up to the roots of my hair.

Our eyes connect again, and before I know what I'm doing, I lift myself off the chair.

He springs out of his, as though he was waiting for me to move first, and then we stand toe to toe. I can feel his eyes on the top of my head, I'm unable to look at him just yet. I close my eyes and lean forward, pressing my forehead to his solid chest.

His fingers cradle the base of my neck. My chin quivers when the tears start. His other hand comes around my waist and pulls me closer, pressing me into his body from head to toe. He is warm, and solid, and beautiful.

"Shhhh," he whispers close to my ear.

I hadn't realized those tears became sobs, gut wrenching sobs. I'm crying because of him—the loss of him. I may not have a soul, but my heart loves him.

Eight

Zachary

I can't help myself; I am utterly lost in this connection. My mouth moves around her head, leaving kisses in its wake. Over her hair, down her ear, collecting the tears from her cheeks and chin. She tilts her head and I seize the opportunity to taste her throat, then I come back up toward her mouth, hovering so close I can almost feel it, our breath mingling together through our open, gasping mouths.

She moves, tasting my lip with the tip of her tongue and that is enough to push me over the edge. I am ravenous for her. Hungry.

"Can you even do this?" she asks.

It has been so long, and never after my death. "I sure as fuck hope so." I push my hardness into her to show her my desperate need to try.

She wraps her arms around my neck and pulls me against her. We kiss hard, and eager; no rhythm, just hungry for each other.

I give over all control and just let my body feel every sensation that had been forgotten, neglected or left behind. Having her both surrender *to* me, and take *from* me has me lightheaded and dizzy.

She practically climbs my body, wrapping her legs around my waist, pressing her heat against mine. Grinding. *Oh, fuck, the grinding.*

My hands find a purpose and it happens to be to touch every inch of her body, thin from depression's starvation. I try to reign myself in, scared I might hurt her.

I carry her up the stairs and into her room, laying her back onto the mattress, I pull away from her mouth to work on taking her clothes off. I pull her pants down her legs and kiss my way up her body; lifting her shirt over her head on my way. "Beautiful."

Nine

May

Oh, my god. My body is tingling, absolutely humming with anticipation. I can barely hear my heavy breaths over the pounding rush pulsing in my ears. I reach for his shirt and tug it up. He stops me, pushing my arms away and pulling back. "I want to see you," I plead.

I watch him struggle with some internal dilemma. I wait for him as patiently as I can, but it is too long. I climb to my knees in front of where he is standing, so I can pull him back into me.

I wrap my arms around his neck and kiss him sweetly on top of his forehead, on both eye lids, and then across from one cheek to the other, planting little kisses on the corners of his lips and then both top and bottom. I slide my arms down to the hem of his shirt again and run my fingers up his chest.

His face contorts in agony, and I feel the reason for his reaction. My fingers brush along tiny, inch-long scars that cover his chest and abdomen—rows of them. I press my lips against his and whisper over and over that he's safe; that he is ok. I follow the lines upward until I have his shirt over his head.

His eyes bulge and I can tell he is still hesitant. I press my naked chest against his in hopes that he can feel my love I run my fingers across his smooth, muscular back and down his arms, where I find they have also been cut. These are deeper, and more ridged—less organized; his forearms have the most damage.

I break away from his mouth and kiss down his neck and across his chest, trying to kiss every inch, every scar, but it seems an impossible feat. I just want to kiss all his pain, no matter how long ago it happened; help ease it. I taste my own salty tears as they fall off my cheeks. My fingers shake, he knows I'm crying, but still I kiss.

 I take his hand and press my lips to his wrist, absorbing all the sadness he had been trying to leach from his own body. Up his forearm, back across his chest and down the other. He wipes my tears off my face and pulls my lips back to his, where I can taste that he has shed his own.

He pulls his pants off and returns me to the bed, making love to me sweeter than I could ever imagine. Loving every inch of my body, showing me more passion than I had ever felt in my entire life. Sharing this moment, with this man—who I can feel loves me more than he can bare, is worth it all. This moment is why I lived. "I love you," I whisper.

"I know," he says, kissing me. "I can feel it. I love you, too."

Ten

Zachary

I watch her as she sleeps. I have never had an experience like that in my life. This woman, who I've got to let go of, to send her to her own death, a death by her own hand, has captivated me and made me wish for more time, more life, more everything.

I run my fingers through her hair and down her body, unable to bring myself to break contact with her skin. She is resting on my chest, her head right over my heart. If she were not here to witness it, it would not be beating. She sees me this way, my old form, because our minds, our vessels, only recognize familiar things. She is familiar with people looking like this, sounding like this, therefore this is me to her. Her brain wouldn't be able to process the alternative, couldn't grasp it.

I instantly regret when my mind shifts to the inevitable. I feel like I might die from what she has to do. I feel like I'm being selfish right now, having her sleep while her soul is lost and fighting to stay bright. Every second is a risk. But I am selfish, and I need this. I need her in my arms, on my chest, in my heart.

Guilt finally forces me into action. Even though I feel equally guilty over having to make her kill herself, I know, at least, that one is for her *own* good.

"May…May, love…you have to wake up now," I whisper into her ear.

She shifts and pulls her arm tightly around my chest, hugging me. My throat chokes with sadness.

"Come on, sweet girl, wake up." I kiss her hair, breathing in her smell. Never wanting to go another day without it, I hold on to it while I can.

"Why?"

"Don't make me say it, ok?"

She stiffens a little and I know she understands what my words mean. She takes a deep breath and lifts her head up, leaning on her elbow, looking deep within my eyes. "Are you going to be able to be with me?"

"Yes," I croak

"I've thought about how I should do it; I think going over the bridge is too hard now. I feel like I would be leaving you. I'd rather stay here and die while you hold me. Is that too much? Would it be too hard for you?"

I can't speak, I just shake my head. *Fuck*. I need to do this for her. For me, even. I couldn't let her plummet to her death like that. I will do everything in my power to keep her comfortable and loved, and not feeling alone.

Eleven

May

He follows me into the bathroom. I feel heartbroken by all of this, but I know I will only make it harder on him, who I have asked to witness this, so I try and be as brave as I can manage.

I've pulled a long t-shirt on, trying to achieve a little modesty for whoever has to find my body. The old me creeps in and tells myself it will probably be the landlord when I stop paying the rent—that no one else would care.

But I see Zachary, and know that if I had met him in another situation, he *would* have cared. He *would* have found me. Hell, I might not have even be in this predicament. So I find happiness in that. It may be too late for our living selves to be together, but I trust him, and believe we will be connected even after I do this—in some way or another.

He sits in the bathtub and I climb in after him, laying my back on his chest, feeling his breath on my neck. I swallow the knot in my throat that wants me to choke. I take a shaky breath and tell him that I love him, feeling his chest shake, I know he can't tell me back right now. I know he is crying for me, maybe for himself, too. We are both losing each other right now. His squeezing arms held tightly around me tell me enough, and I bask in his unspoken love.

I turn my head around to kiss him, and for a long moment we sit here frozen, fused by our mouths. His tears, mixing with mine.

I turn around again when I feel like I might change my mind. I think about just saying 'fuck it' to my soul and live with him until it dies in the darkness, however long that may be. But I know he wouldn't let me. He wouldn't let my soul die.

Taking a deep breath, "Goodbye, my sweet Zachary. Here's to being connected to you in the afterlife." I drag my straight razor down my wrist, deeper than I ever had, slicing through every cut I had made before. The familiar goosebumps trickle across my skin.

I hear him distantly in the background telling me all the sweet words a person craves to hear.

I'm struggling with my mission, trying to do the other side, but I know I can't, I've cut so deep my nerves are severed, I can't grip the blade right now.

I'm lost in the flow of blood leaving my body. There's so much of it pulsing out of me with every heartbeat. I feel myself start to shake, my teeth chatter. I'm mumbling something through my shock. I'm trying to say I love him. I don't know if it's coming out audible through all the shivers.

He pulls me tighter; I feel his embrace. I hear him tell me he loves me…clear as day, I can hear him. The shivers are gone. The cold is gone. I must be gone.

Twelve

Zachary

I know the instant she is lost to me here; I feel her soul recharge and head on course. I hold her body, the only thing of her I have left. I cry every ounce of tears I kept trapped for her sake. My chest aches with loss, my heart, broken.

I don't know how long I sit here; we go by a different frame of time once you're dead. Rigor mortis has set in, so I know it's been hours. I move from under her stiff body and pull myself free of the tub.

"My beautiful May."

That woman, who never had anyone care about her her entire life, had shown me more love than I thought possible. That girl who shouldn't know how to, loved so fiercely it changed me. She has left an imprint on me larger than anything in my previous life.

I don't know what to do anymore, I can't feel her light any longer; she is on her path now, and I am lost on mine without her.

Thirteen

May

I know exactly what he means now, about being connected to everything. I feel it in my figurative bones. I don't actually have bones anymore but I don't know how else to explain it—the sensation, it's deep.

I feel everything, and nothing, all at the same time. If I think something, I feel it, when I feel it, I love it.

The light I know to follow is leading me somewhere.

Zachary said it would be hard, the things I have to do, so I prepare myself for my arrival and what's awaiting me when I get there. In the mean time I am happy to be.

***

I'm stunned when I see my father's face. Out of nowhere, I am at home. My father is leaving. This is the night I discovered he did not love me. The night I first learned crushing-heartbreak.

He is standing at the door. My perspective now different than it was when it happened all those years ago.

I have a better idea of what this means now that I'm older. I'm not seeing this through child eyes. I kind of wish I was, because the look on his face is more crushing than I recall.

He looks excited. That *fucker* is excited to leave me; to be with his new woman. There is no remorse.

There was a time I'd convinced myself that had he lived longer, he may have come back, begging for forgiveness, and asking to be my dad again. I don't see any of that. He is *eager* to leave. Probably why he wrapped his car around the tree before he even got to her. *Serves him right.*

I see my mother here, too. She is yelling at him—which I don't remember happening originally. I can't make out what she's saying. I don't feel it is pertinent to this, so I turn back to him.

I can't understand what I'm supposed to do here. What I need to do to move forward. I just want to be out of here, but I know I can't leave.

I'm in some sort of loop. I see him walk from the bedroom to the front door hundreds of times. I can't see what I am supposed to see—what I'm obviously missing.

I can't un-hate him. I can't let it go. I can't breathe from the sadness that he didn't love me. I *can't*.

I feel the weight of this so heavily I can't think. I sit and watch my mother, her mouth forming the words I can't hear, loop after loop, hypnotized.

"I will tell her you hate her... tell her you left her... fuck you, you'll never know her." My mother's words hit me hard, like a punch to the chest. Not that I'm surprised she is capable of such cruelty, she is *plenty* capable. But I don't know what this means.

I focus on her words and watch my father's face as he hears them. I see the pain in his eyes as they hit their mark. And then I *really* watch, which is when the look comes again; the one that I thought was excitement. He looks at me... the six-year-old me—the one hidden behind the recliner. "My girl will know you're lying." And my six-year-old self peeks her little head around the armrest and nods in confirmation to him, and he smiles the little side-smile I remember about him, before I hated him.

My heart rips open with the guilt. And I realize my mother had twisted the memory of this day so intricately that I thought something completely different had happened. I close my eyes and let it go. The pain, the heartache, the torment and torture this has caused my whole life.

I forgive my father.

***

The light is back and I am following it again. I feel lighter, and somehow heavier at the same time.

I can forgive my father for wanting to leave my mother, I can forgive, knowing now, that he would have kept me in his life. He would have loved me.

The weight comes from one more thing my mother did to ruin my life. And I know firsthand none of these little walk-throughs are going to prove otherwise, she's a monster.

Then, as though I conjured her into my mind, my mother is standing in front of me. Not me from today, the me who is young, the me who has just been beaten by her angry mother for making her boyfriend want to look at me. The me who could not do anything *but* wrong. The me who didn't want that man's attention, but who got it anyway, and then got more of her mother's hatred.

"You little slut," I hear her say, spittle hitting little May on my face with the venomous words. "You whore, I bet you let him touch you, didn't you?!"

I watch myself shake my head; I hadn't let him do anything.

This was the first time I had been truly afraid to be in this house, really scared that something could happen to me. I had screamed, terrified of the man in my room.

He had snuck in and startled me awake. I thought yelling for my mother, even though she was evil, was the safest thing. It did stop him, but I took a beating from her for tempting him.

Yes, little sleeping girls are so *tempting.*

I remember this day, I had always known she hated me, but this was the day I learned how deep it was seated. She didn't care what that man could have done to me, she cared only that he wanted me *instead* of her.

I handle this one better than the one with my father, I am very familiar with this form of torment. I go into my favorite state; numb. And I let my mother's words hit me like they had most my life. I don't shed a tear; I don't let her win. Which is something I can't say for younger me; she still hasn't perfected that trick yet. I resent her a little for giving our mother that power with her tears, her pleading and begging to be heard—to be loved.

I sit and stare, first at my mother, who is fuming, selling all her hate and anger. Then at myself, who is just absorbing it, feeling it, letting her say those things, letting it actually *affect* her.

I *hate* her.

I might hate little May more than I hate my mother. The *stupid* way she just sits there wishing her mommy loved her. *Fucking idiot.* I'd hit her too.

I revel in that hatred, and then it dawns on me, this one is not about my mother. This is about me, and my inability to love myself. I take a deep breath, so deep my chest aches when it's forced to expel so much air. With shaky lungs I try and calm myself with slower, more rhythmic breaths.

I look again at little May, tormented by life, coping as best she can while being naive in her youth. I choose to forgive her, to give her peace and love. To know she did her best to survive, even when the world gave her nothing.

I wipe tears off of my cheeks, tears for myself, tears for the life I always should have had, and the love I should have felt. I will give it to myself, I will love me every day. I will say only nice things to myself, and I will give me what no one else has… peace.

***

I'm out here again, wandering, just being everywhere; everything.

I can see the beckoning light and I follow it, sure that nothing could be more painful and triumphant than the last trial, I almost *will* it to happen quicker; eager to be done with all of this.

And just like that, I regret it. Vomit flows into my mouth and it spews from the bottom of my stomach. I choke and cough until I have nothing left, and then I heave until I ache. Hyperventilating with the effort.

The man in front of me, my step-father, the man who took from me what I can never give another. The man who stole my innocence, my self, and my soul. The man I carve out from my skin. The man whose hands I can feel on my body when it's quiet and I should be sleeping—the fear of waking with his groping fingers on me keeping me awake.

Even though I'm older now, and know they aren't coming for me anymore, I know they don't have that reach, he still haunts me.

I can't look at him. Thousands of loops have passed by, and each time I tell myself I need to do this. This has to be the finale. I don't have anything worse than this, this is my shame, my hate, my pain.

I watch little May; she is curled inside her blankets; she has burrito-ed herself inside. I remember thinking it would be harder to touch me if he had to go through the trouble of unwrapping me—maybe he would go away. But he never did, no matter how many layers I had, he always made it through.

This is one out of a hundred times; I can't pin point what makes this one different. I look at him now, with the eyes of an adult. He is disgusting, repulsive, a deviant.

He watches younger me inside those blankets, obviously plotting, reveling in the situation. I can see how eager he is to attack that little girl.

The scene is only this: May under the covers, on top of her mattress that sits in the corner of the room on the floor.

The predator, a few feet inside the room, hand over the bulge in his pants.

I retch again, the muscles in my stomach constrict and I heave nothingness.

I squeeze my eyes shut, trying to un-see that, trying to forget what that means for little May. I cry. I cry until I can't cry anymore, until I am exhausted and aching; my face swollen with grief, my chest on fire.

I pull my eyes open, still unable to turn them toward him. Instead, I focus on the door behind him; an escape from this scene. I stare blankly at the opening; countless loops are passing. I'm readying myself to look again at the players in the room when something stops me.

It's dark in the hallway, the nightlight inside my old room making it even darker out the door, but I know my eyes aren't lying, they aren't wrong. I see my mother's face hidden in the blackness. I turn before I can let my brain understand what that means. Too scared to go down that path, I lie to myself and tell me that I was wrong, that there is something else in this room, and that I need to make more of an attempt to see it. I stared too long, and thought too much, and saw something that wasn't there.

I look at May not moving. Thirty loops. I can't even see the blankets rise or fall with her breath; she is still.

I look at him, I stare at him—angry at him for not giving me the answers I want from this. Save for the nineteen times he blinks and the three times he constricts his hand around his bulge, he doesn't move.

I'm more afraid now of the doorway than I was to initially see his face again.

I watch the room as a whole, losing count how many times. It's almost too hard to know where the start and end differentiate in the loop. All of it blurs together.

I am numb to what is in the room. Pulse steady, I drag my attention back to the door, my eyes fall right to the spot in question—my mother's face. Gasping as it finally becomes real, I let the horror of it wash over me. The hatred I have had for my mother all of these years intensifies beyond a manageable level.

I force a steadying breath and watch the doorway to see what there is to see. My room is along the hallway, so she is actually leaning against the wall across from my door, resting her back against it; arms folded across her chest. She looks annoyed, her irritated scowl prominent along her brow.

I notice her mouth moves for a few words. Like the other time I can't actually hear them yet. I focus on deciphering them; over and over I watch. I start to hear a hissing sound… no, a whisper.

Closing my eyes to sharpen my hearing, "Jesus…" I clearly hear her say. I settle my jumping heart back down so I can hear the rest without struggling to listen over the pounding.

"Jesus…" I hear again. "Fuck…" I hear, as well. I don't know where it falls in the sentence, yet. I open my eyes to see her mouth forming the words. 'Jesus' is unquestionably the start of her sentence.

"Jesus… something," I catch myself saying aloud.

I close my eyes again, time ticks by. I hear her say those words over and over. Getting lost in the cadence of them, they lull me into a patterned tempo. I can hear them louder now; having extracted any and all things unnecessary.

And then, they are clear, the words that will haunt me, I'm sure, forever. "Jesus… just fuck her already and come to bed."

My knees buckle. I fall hard to the ground. Her words come out faster now, clear enough that she could be whispering them into my ear.

My head hits the floor hard as I double over in pain—physical, debilitating, pain. Her words strike me like her fists never could, crushing me.

I dig my fingers into the roots of my hair and pull. I pull so hard I can hear the Velcro sound of the follicles releasing. Adrenaline pumps through my veins as the hatred floods. I pull so hard my fingers ache, the strands of hair biting into my skin as it weaves more tightly around.

My arms shake, my jaw clenches, my breath heaves like a rabid dog. I can feel the spit push through my teeth, seething, my hatred turning me into a beast. I grind my forehead into the carpet, trying to push my head into the floor, I scream, I scream so fucking hard my throat bleeds.

Sitting up, I pull my hands from my hair and spit on the floor, I spit again when I realize I can still taste my bloody hatred.

I focus on the pounding in my head, matching beats with the throb of my fingers. The ache giving me that familiar feeling; the endorphins leveling me.

I'm washed over with the feeling of love, just then. I try and extract where that love is coming from. I feel it like a flood, I feel it in my veins; pumping the hatred out until I'm replenished.

I rack my brain for answers. Tears fall from my chin; I wipe them away only for more to come. My body is humming, the beat of my heart slowing and changing, my own beats become distant.

In the foreground I hear the new ones. I focus on them, on the love, on the things I want to feel.

I let go of that room, that room and every time that scenario repeated itself throughout my years. Plucking each time out of my head and flinging it into oblivion. Throwing every feeling it evoked, all the hatred, pain, confusion, sadness and shame; all of it gone.

I focus on my new heartbeat, on my new destination; one that is not heavy with my old life. Transcending all that pain, free-falling into a forever where that is not me, that will not define me. I find peace in letting go.

I'm not falling anymore, but I don't open my eyes, yet. I want to stay here in my peacefulness. I want to bask in all that it means for me. To truly worship it.

I breathe a sigh, grateful for having come out on the other side of those things—albeit dead, I'm at peace. Life is the longest thing we do *while* we are alive, but this I will do longer, *eternally*. I am ok with all my lifetime of pain, because *this* is forever.

I let that feeling put a smile on my face, no more resentment, hatred, anger or regret. None of it matters now.

I feel only the warmth of my happiness, the glowing brightness of my soul expanding to the point of explosion, and I laugh. The sound is light, and echoes throughout my new world. I feel everything respond to me, all with their tinkling little laughs, sharing in my happiness.

I'm floored by the gravity of oneness I feel. Opening my eyes to welcome in my new sight, I see everything is different, yet somehow familiar.

I am on my bridge, I know that, but it's a different bridge, nothing about it is the same, but I know this is the one.

I walk to the edge. Running water flows under this one, where mine had had a dirt covered valley. The metal guard rail from my memory replaced by this rickety, wooden one. I run my fingers along it and notice that my hand is new, too. My knuckles aren't scarred from pounding my fists, my wrists are not marred. My skin has not a spot of imperfection. It's practically glowing.

I look down to my feet, my body is different too, I'm no longer the emaciated girl I was, I am healthy looking, and taller than I remember; the distance seeming grater to my feet than before.

I put my hands to my face, trying to trace all the features of it. My nose—button-like, my lips—different, but still small, and I am ok with that. My eyes are doll like now, big circles instead of the almond-shape from before. My ears, in perfect symmetrical placement. My hair, combed and running over my shoulders; light brown from what I can see. A beautiful color. I run my fingers through it, no longer feeling the pain of trying to scalp myself.

Pleased with my own new look, I take in the rest of my new world. There are people here, I notice now. It seems if I focus on something I am able to see it, or feel it, but if I don't, it just becomes muddled—or rather, blurred. As though I don't have to be aware if I don't choose to; I can just be. I don't have to take a form, but I can.

I focus on the people as individuals. I can see the expressions on their faces, the human emotions, the ones that make me cringe a little if I focus too hard on them. One in particular looks different than the rest. He is tall, thin, but muscular; dark hair, yellow-green eyes. His face is smooth looking, but for the spotting of hair across his jaw. He is leaning against a light post that is new to my bridge as well. His hands hooked in the loops of his pants. One ankle crossed over the other, looking more relaxed than the rest of the people.

I feel my feet take me toward him, wanting a closer look. I focus on him and only him, the periphery of my vision goes dark, leaving nothing but him. I watch his blinking eyes, his breathing chest, hearing his steady breath, although I am still yards away from him.

I hear his heart, the pattern of it mesmerizing me. I walk closer still, and I can hear the hum of his body, the mechanics of it working. I watch him turn his head and catch the instant his eyes lock onto mine.

Fourteen
Many years later

Zachary

It was so lonely for so long without my sweet May. I became lost for a period. I found hope again through helping the suicide souls cross, I buried myself in it. But I realized they didn't need me like she had.

Not a day has finished without being full of thoughts of our days together. The love that grew in such a desperate time. I can feel content, almost, with just having known her.

Being able to share ourselves with each other when we weren't able to have a bond like that with anyone before has altered me. Even though it was just a brief time, it changed me. Knowing her soul is in peace, and remains a part of me now, is the only way I keep going.

I'm watching the people on the bridge today: a mother with her children, a man reading the paper on a bench, couples holding hands. A sudden pull urges me to turn. The face meeting my gaze startles me. People shouldn't be able to see me, and yet, I know this one does.

I shuffle my feet and stand facing her. We don't break eye contact as both of us begin to move toward each other.

"Zachary," I hear her tiny voice say, hesitantly.

"May?" I can't imagine how this is possible, how she's able to be on my version of the bridge, but here she is.

Against all odds she has found me. I know that, despite the impossible, my sweet May has done the unfathomable She defied everything, and in the mix of all the millions of tiny twinkling lights, she has found mine.

I go to her, wrapping my arms around her new body. I squeeze her so tightly we hum like the rim of crystal.

Our mouths find each other's and I kiss her with all the love I'm filled with. I can hear in the distance as the hum engulfs us all, and we sound like a symphony of love.

"I love you, my beautiful May," I say into her mouth, not wanting to break the connection, but needing to verbalize to her.

Her grin is so big, I kiss her teeth. I love the feel of her happiness. I kiss around her lips, then dance with her tongue as she offers it again. I am blissful.

Fifteen

May

I knew it was him the second I caught sight of his eyes. I had found him.

The love in his heart, the rhythm of it, being what pulled me from my final trauma—one I might not have gotten through otherwise. His heartbeat sounded the alarm for safety, flooding my veins with his love and washing my past away. Becoming *his* world. Literally.

We stand together, fused by our mouths and hands. Nights and days pass around us on our bridge. People come and go, replacing one another in the background.

Time moves differently for me now, it's both slower and faster, depending on where my focus is. And although I get to spend an eternity with my Zachary, I want it moving agonizingly slow. I want to bask in every sluggish second with him.

Epilogue

May

We had finally been able to dislodge our physical selves from each other and have found a passion for traveling. Simply moving around the aethers together, seamlessly.

Our love was not meant for the living world. He was born and dead before I was even a thought, we never would have met then. So our pain, and subsequent suicides, are what led us to find each other.

I am grateful every day that I lived in misery for my short life. I realize it was worth every second—I'd do it hundreds of times with the knowledge of finding him to be with for my eternity.

"I *fucking* love you," I say to him.

"So *fucking* much, babe."

More from the author

[Collecting Rayne Volume 1](#)
[Degenerate](#)
[The Boy](#)
[The Embalmer](#)
[XXX](#)
[My Christmas Story](#)
[Devour](#)
[Retaliation](#)
[App](#)

[Collecting Rayne Volume 2](#)

[Boys Will Be Boys](#)

[The Other Place](#)

[Tantalize](#)

[Killstreme](#)

[Daddy Issues](#)

[Necrosis](#)

About the author

Rayne lives in the Arizona desert, free to leave her house whenever she wants, she chooses not to risk death by sweltering sun demons. Instead, she stays safely indoors with a computer and all the words she knows, slapping them together in any which way she chooses in the moment.

Often gory, sometimes erotic. She loves the limitless boundaries of writing, and tends to push them toward extreme.

Made in United States
Orlando, FL
27 November 2024

54539681R00040